Emmy
the Exaggerating
Elephant

Fenton
the Fearful Frog

Gertie
the Grungy Goat

the Happy
Hamster

the Impatient
Iguana

Ollie
the Obedient
Ostrich

Perry
the Polite
Porcupine

Queenie
the Quiet Quail

Rupert
the Resourceful
Rhinoceros

Ziggy
the Zippy Zebra

Yori
the Yucky Yak

Xavier
the X-ploring
Xenops

Wendy
the Wise
Woodchuck

NOTE TO PARENTS

Bradley and the Great Swamp Mystery
A story about bravery

In this story, Bradley the Brave Bear and his AlphaPet friends decide to have a picnic at the Great Swamp despite the rumor of a Swamp Monster and the prediction of a summer storm. When one of the AlphaPets gets lost, Bradley's calm manner and bravery help save the day.

In addition to enjoying this adventure with your child, you can use it to teach a gentle lesson about the important value of bravery — being courageous, loyal, and doing what one thinks is right.

You can use this story to introduce the letter **B**. As you read about Bradley the Brave Bear, ask your child to listen for all the **B** words and point to the objects whose names begin with **B**. When you've finished reading the story, your child will enjoy doing the activity at the end of the book.

The AlphaPets™ characters were conceived and created by Ruth Lerner Perle.
Characters interpreted and designed by Deborah Colvin Borgo.
Cover design by the Antler & Baldwin Design Group.
Book design and production by Publishers' Graphics, Inc.
Logo design by Deborah Colvin Borgo and Nancy S. Norton.

Printed and Manufactured in the United States of America

Bradley and the Great Swamp Mystery

RUTH LERNER PERLE

Illustrated by Deborah Colvin Borgo

Grolier Enterprises Inc.   Danbury, Connecticut

One hot summer day, Bradley the Brave Bear was meeting his AlphaPet friends for a picnic at Old Great Swamp.

Ziggy the Zippy Zebra arrived early. "Hey there, Ziggy," called Bradley. "It's a good thing you take vitamins! That basket looks mighty heavy."

"It sure is," said Ziggy. "It's full of bread, bologna, bananas, and big bottles of blueberry soda. And I even brought my banjo."

   Soon Perry the Polite Porcupine arrived exactly on time, as usual.

   "Good morning, Bradley, good morning, Ziggy," he called, tipping his hat. "Thank you so much for inviting me. But I must tell you that a rainstorm is predicted for this afternoon."

   Bradley looked up at the sky. "I don't think it will rain," he said. "And even if it does, we'll manage."

Then Fenton the Fearful Frog and Ivy the Impatient Iguana arrived.

"I'm afraid we're a little late," Fenton said. "I had to pack my bandages, my insect spray, my sewing kit, my flashlight and my toothbrush—just in case.

It's going to rain, you know. Are you sure we should go on this picnic? Will we get wet? Will we catch cold? Will we be hurt?"

Ivy hopped up and down. "Enough talk!" she shouted. "Let's go! Let's go! I can't wait another minute! What are we waiting for?"

"I suppose you're all waiting for me," called Lizzy the Lazy Lamb as she walked slowly up the path. "Sorry I'm late, but I was tired and sat down to rest."

TO OLD GREAT SWAMP
Beware the Monster!

"Well, I guess we're ready to go now," said Bradley. "Follow me!"

When they came to the water, everybody helped spread the blankets and set out the food. It was very quiet except for the buzzing of bees and the chirping of crickets.

"I wonder why no one else is picnicking here," said Fenton.

"They're probably afraid of the monster," said Ziggy.

"Wha...what monster?" Fenton asked, looking around him.

"The Great Swamp Monster," declared
Ziggy. He pointed to a pile of rocks. "He
lives behind those rocks, and when it
gets dark, he comes out and makes
scary sounds: *whoo, whooo...*"

"I beg your pardon, but there's no such thing as monsters," said Perry.

"There is, too!" said Fenton.

"I don't believe there is," Perry said politely.

"Is, too!" insisted Ziggy.

"Calm down," said Bradley. "Even if there *is* a monster, we don't have to worry. We'll all be safely at home by the time it gets dark."

"Monster, shmonster!" said Ivy. "Pass the sandwiches and the soda *please*, I'm hungry and I want to eat!"

So the AlphaPets sat down on their blankets.

Perry folded a napkin carefully and spread it on his knee. He placed a sandwich on a plate, cut it neatly in half, and took small bites. Then he poured himself some soda and took small sips.

Fenton helped himself to a bun. Then he emptied his "just-in-case" bag and checked to make sure nothing had been lost.

Ziggy tuned his banjo while he sipped his soda.

Lizzy fell asleep while
eating a bunch of grapes.

Bradley finished his sandwich and lay on his back
looking up at the sky. He pretended that the grey
clouds were puffy little dinosaurs.

Ivy gobbled her sandwich up and gulped her soda down.

"Let's go!" she called. "What's taking so long? I'm ready to go hiking!"

But nobody else wanted to rush.

So Ivy grabbed her butterfly net, tightened her hiking boots, and went off into the woods alone.

Bradley watched as Ivy disappeared behind some bramble bushes. Then he looked back up at the sky. The clouds seemed to be getting darker.

Splat!
Bradley felt a drop of rain on his forehead.

Then, *plink!* A raindrop bounced on Ziggy's banjo.

Drip!

Drip!

Drip!

Rain sprinkled down on Fenton's bag.

Boom! The sound of thunder rumbled in the distance.

Crack! Lightning zig-zagged across the dark sky.

Fenton started to tremble.

"Oh my, oh my, it's really dark now and I think I hear the monster coming," he cried.

"That's only thunder," said Bradley. "We'd better make a tent out of these blankets."

Bradley woke Lizzy, and they all crawled into the blanket tent together.

"What about Ivy?" Perry wanted to know. "Why isn't she back yet?"

"The monster will get her for sure," said Ziggy.

"Yes," whispered Fenton. "The monster will get us all if we don't leave here right away."

Bradley was worried about Ivy too, but he forced himself to smile.

"I have an idea," he said, trying to look cheerful. "Ziggy, play us a happy tune on your banjo. Perry, you sing along. I'll go out and look for Ivy."

"But what about the rain, the thunder, the lightning,
and the MONSTER?" said Fenton. "Aren't you scared?"

"I guess I am a little," admitted Bradley. "But I can't
let that stop me. Ivy may be in trouble. I have to help
her."

Bradley buckled his boots and went out into the rain. He ran down to the lake. The ground felt squishy and slimy and slippery.

He looked behind every bush, and up and down the path. But Ivy was nowhere to be seen.

"Ivy! Ivy!" he shouted.

There were dark shadows on the swampy water, and over on the rock pile, Bradley saw a strange shape! Was it the Great Swamp Monster?

Bradley's heart was beating, *thump, thump, thump*.

Suddenly, Bradley heard a faint cry.

"Help! Help! Somebody please help me!"

The sound came from the rock pile.

It sounded like Ivy!

"Hold on, Ivy!" Bradley called. "I'm coming!"

Bradley made his way through the puddles and around the rocks.

And there was Ivy, cold and wet and trembling.

"Oh, Bradley, am I glad to see you!" she cried. "I tripped over the rocks and hurt my ankle. I'm afraid I can't walk."

"Lean on me. I'll help you back," said Bradley.

When the AlphaPets saw Bradley and Ivy coming down the path, they cheered and clapped and shouted *Hooray!*

Suddenly everyone noticed the rain had stopped! Everything was quiet again. The sun came out from behind the clouds and shone through the last glistening raindrops. And in the sky above the rock pile, the most beautiful rainbow appeared.

"That's Bradley's rainbow!" cried Ivy.

"Bradley is our hero!"

"Yes," everybody agreed. "Bradley's the bravest bear there ever was!"

Be brave with me and learn these words.

bird

book

banjo

basket

ball

bottle

bat

boat

butterfly

bananas

Look back at the pictures in this book and try to find these and other things that begin with the letter B.

Aa Bb

Gg Hh

Mm Nn Oo Pp

Uu Vv Ww